This Wee Book Belongs to

Aster

....

....

Sean Steell

"To all the staff at the North Gateway Café"

Rupert the Red Squirrel
First published in Great Britain in 2024
Paperback ISBN 978-1-7396790-0-2

Illustration and Book design by: www.happydesigner.co.uk

Rupert the Red Squirrel

By Sam Steele

Doodled by Sarah-Leigh Wills

Away in the north at Daviot Woods
Is a cute little café with traybakes so good
In the trees right behind, lived Rupert the squirrel
As red as can be and his tail had a curl

The staff all loved Rupert, especially Melissa
Who worked every day as a first-rate barista
It was good when Emma or Jenny was there
But Melissa was best as they had the same hair

And when it was quiet and she had a break
To the feeder, for Rupert, some nuts she would take
Rupert loved these and was happy to chat
But when at the feeder he would never be sat

Sometimes without notice young Rupert would flee
And was gone in a jiffy up the nearest tall tree
Melissa was sorry she did not get to say
A goodbye to Rupert before he went on his way

She'd return to the counter where work would begin
To serve the next guest, a cute doggie named Finn
Now Finn was a boisterous black cocker spaniel
Often a handful for his best friend named Daniel

When Emma saw him, her hand Finn would lick
At breaks she would throw him a ball or a stick
But she said to Melissa that she always found
If Finn was nearby there was no Rupert around

The next time Melissa was out for a chat
Before Rupert dashed off, she asked him if that
There was a reason that he skurried away
Before Melissa, a good bye, had managed to say

Rupert went quiet and looked really shy
But managed to say he was scared which is why
He ran up a tree because in the end
He thought the big monster could not be his friend

This frightened Melissa and she was aghast
With fear in her voice of Rupert she asked
"What terrible creature do you think I should
Be careful of when I am about in the woods"

"A Black Monster. It's huge (well much bigger than me)
And if you saw it, you would be sure to agree
The thing at the back is for whipping and fighting
And the bit at the front is for snarling and biting"

This frightened Melissa who was scared to go out
In case the black creature was prowling about
She passed on this news to Emma and Jen
And said to the forest she would not go again

Emma replied with a bit of a grin
"It isn't a monster but the doggie named Finn
When you see Rupert the next time you are out
Say there's nothing he needs to be worried about"

Melissa soon realised that she had been silly
When thinking of Rupert, she asked herself, Will he
Accept what she said and then in the end
Consider that Finn could become a new friend?

She knew it was strange to try something new
And starting a friendship is a hard thing to do
She suggested that Rupert go out on a limb
And see if Finn might be a good friend to him

"But he's big and he's jumpy, with a whip and a scowl
And I'm frightened of him so tell me please how'll
I start to be friends if his name I don't know
Because not even once I have said an hello"

"Look the bit at the back is not for whipping and fighting
But he wags it to show that he thinks you are exciting
And the bit at the front when it barks makes a din
But it shows you he's happy with an extra big grin"

"So first check with a parent, or teacher, or nan
If it's okay to make friends and if they say that you can
He won't know your name so first you should say"
"Hi my name's Rupert, have you had a nice day?"

Rupert was nervous and more than just shy
He was feeling quite anxious and he wanted to fly
But he trusted Melissa and thought he should show
He could pluck up the courage and give it a go

"Hi my name's Rupert, have you had a nice day?
I was wondering if you knew a game we could play"
"Hi Rupert I'm Finn" he said with a smile
"I have been wanting to talk to you for a while"

"I'd love to be friends, Daniel says its okay
As long as we don't wander too far away"
Finn looked really happy and so very soon
The two became friends and played all afternoon

So when ever young Finn heads to the café
Young Rupert is not seen to be running away
Rupert's glad he said 'Hi' because in the end
He is not scared of a monster but he has a new friend

Other books by Sam Steele

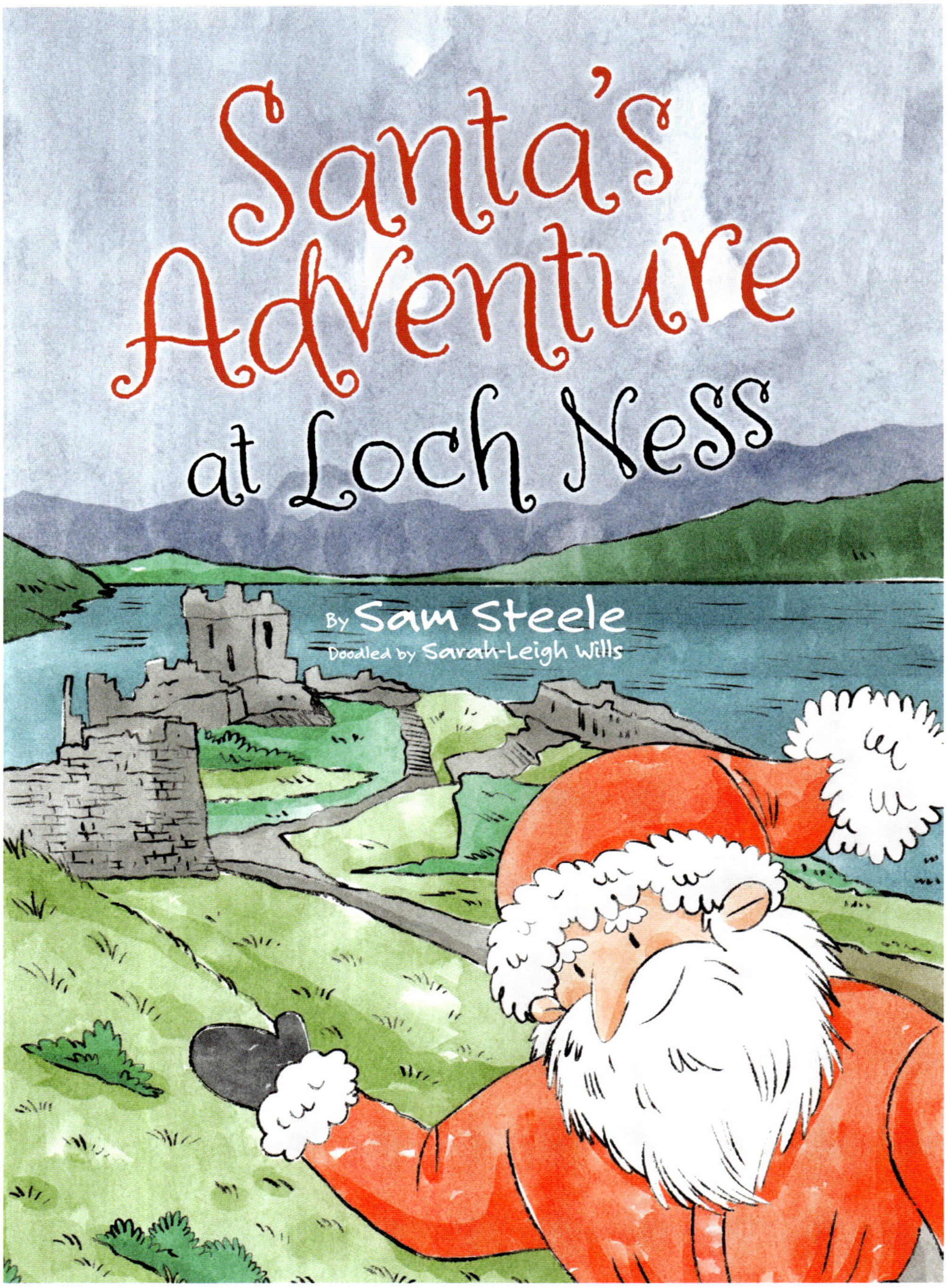

Get your paws on a copy:

www.samsteelepoet.co.uk